For two pirates-in-training:
Myra the Bold and
Sterling the Brave
N.G.

For Lyra
C.R.

BLOOMSBURY CHILDREN'S BOOKS
Bloomsbury Publishing Plc
50 Bedford Square, London, WC1B 3DP, UK
29 Earlsfort Terrace, Dublin 2, Ireland

BLOOMSBURY, BLOOMSBURY CHILDREN'S BOOKS and the Diana logo are trademarks of Bloomsbury Publishing Plc

First published in Great Britain 2020 by Bloomsbury Publishing Plc
This edition published in Great Britain 2021 by Bloomsbury Publishing Plc

Text copyright © Neil Gaiman, 2020
Illustrations copyright © Chris Riddell, 2020

Neil Gaiman and Chris Riddell have asserted their right under the Copyright, Designs and Patents Act, 1988, to be identified as the Author and Illustrator of this work

A catalogue record for this book is available from the British Library

ISBN PB: 978-1-5266-1471-1; ISBN Waterstones: 978-1-5266-4274-5; ISBN eBook: 978-1-5266-1470-4

2 4 6 8 10 9 7 5 3 1

Printed and bound in China by C&C Offset Printing Co Ltd, Shenzhen, Guangdong

FSC
www.fsc.org
MIX
Paper from
responsible sources
FSC® C008047

To find out more about our authors and books visit www.bloomsbury.com and sign up for our newsletters

NEIL GAIMAN

PIRATE
STEW

ILLUSTRATED BY
CHRIS RIDDELL

BLOOMSBURY
CHILDREN'S BOOKS
LONDON OXFORD NEW YORK NEW DELHI SYDNEY

Pirate Stew! Pirate Stew!
Pirate Stew for me and you!

The night my mum and dad went out
I said, "We won't be babysat!"
They said, "You must not grump and pout.
We're going out and that is that.
We've planned a quite exciting night:
At first we'll dine by candlelight,
then watch a most instructive show
in which we'll learn how flowers grow.
You have to promise to behave."

Then from the hall there came a pitter-
thump. "We know you'll both be brave.
Say hello to your babysitter."

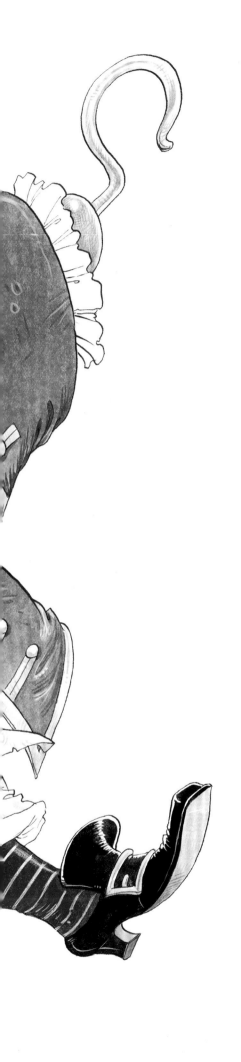

His hair was grey. His face was scarred.

Right leg a peg, left hand a hook.

He grinned a grin and said, "My card."

It read,

Long John McRon
Ship's Cook.

My mum and dad said, "Time to run.
Mr McRon is going to feed you."
Long John said, "Mateys, you have fun
and we will call you if we need you.
Which we will not."

So off they zoomed.
My sister whispered,
"We are doomed."

My parents had not been gone long
when someone knocked upon the door,
and two cracked voices raised in song
were joined by several voices more.

The door was opened. In they came:
A pirate crew. They were not tame.

Now one was fat . . .

. . . and one was thin.

One had a hankie on her head.

One played upon the violin
"Fifteen Bad Men upon a Dead
Man's Chest" and suchlike pirate ditties.

My sister said, "Excuse me, when
is dinner?"

      "Coming soon, my pretties,"
replied a pirate queen. So then,
the pirates headed for the fridge . . .

. . . and gazed inside with puzzled looks.
Some of the pirates scratched their heads.
Some of the pirates sucked their hooks.

"It's difficult to choose," said one.
"Impossible," began another.
"We have to feed 'em," Long John said.
"I told their father and their mother.
 We pirates always keeps our word."
At that each pirate nodded head.
And so they thoughtfully conferred:
"Arr. Beans on toast?" "No beans. No bread."
"Or scrambled eggs?" "Too complicated."
"Spaghetti?" "Looks like worms," one said.
Old Long John thought. He hesitated.

He said, "Me hearties. This is true.
We ought to do what pirates do.
We ought to make a pirate stew!"

Long John produced an ancient pot.
He then produced a wooden spoon.
"We will serve it piping hot
underneath a pirate's moon!"
He beat his spoon against the pan
and with one voice they all began
shouting out most joyfully,
"Now we're back home
from the sea . . .

Pirate Stew! Pirate Stew!
Pirate Stew for me and you!

Pirate Stew! Pirate Stew!
Eat it and you won't be blue.
You can be a *pirate* too!"

. . . half a sack of gold doubloons.

That's the stew that you'll get rich in!"
(Here they danced about the kitchen.)

"Add a haddock, fat or thin,
splice the mainbrace, drop it in!

Tumble in
the smorgasbord,

stir it with
a pirate sword,

season it with mermaid's tears," sang the band of buccaneers.

MERMAID'S
TEARS

"Cannonballs and red bandanas,

pineapples and brown bananas,

locks from Davy Jones's lockers,

blood and thunders, shilling shockers,

add a slice of plank for walking,

and some extra Arrs for talking,

Finally, one ancient codger
said, "I've got a Jolly Roger!"
So he threw that in as well.
Then they rang the dinner bell.

Pirate Stew! Pirate Stew!
Pirate Stew for me and you!
Pirate Stew, Pirate Stew,
eat it and you won't be blue.
You'll become a ***pirate too***!

But my sister said to me,
"If you eat that pirate stew
you'll be what they say you'll be.
You'll become a pirate too."

So we left our bowls of stew.
(Quite unnoticed by the crew,
much too busy chowing down.)
"Now!" they cried. "We'll go to town!"

For the house became piratic.

Sails billowed from the attic.

All the pirates called, "Ahoy!

Raise the anchor, girl and boy."

We went out into the garden,
hauled the anchor off the railing.
"As the moon's above the yardarm,"
called the pirates, "Let's go sailing."

They sailed that house about the town,
they sailed it left, they sailed it right,
they sailed it up, they sailed it down,
they sailed it out into the night.

They sailed our townhouse down the road.
"Old freebooters never stop,"
sang the pirates. Then they spotted
Sally's Little Donut Shop.

"I am closing for the night,"
Sally told them. But the crew
shouted, "We are pirates bright,
here to do what pirates do.
Hand over your donuts, hearties.
We will have **a donut party**."

She said, "They're this morning's donuts,
slightly stale. No need to shout.
Would you like to take and eat them?
Otherwise I'll throw them out."

CLASSIC

ICED

JAM FILLED

TRIPLE SPRINKLE

STAR
SPANGLED

All the pirates cheered so loudly,
threw their hats into the air.
Paid a gold coin, stating proudly,
"Pirates always pay their share."

Donuts jammy, donuts creamy,
donuts chocolate, donuts pale,
donuts yummy, donuts dreamy,
donuts only *slightly* stale.

Me and sister gobbled up a
lot of donuts for our supper.

Then we dropped the pirate crew
beside the Saucy Treasure Chest,
where pirates guzzle rum and do
whatever pirates do the best.
And as Long John steered us homeward,
buccaneers called,

"Toodle-pip!"

Soon we anchored
in our garden,

in our house,

our home,

our ship.

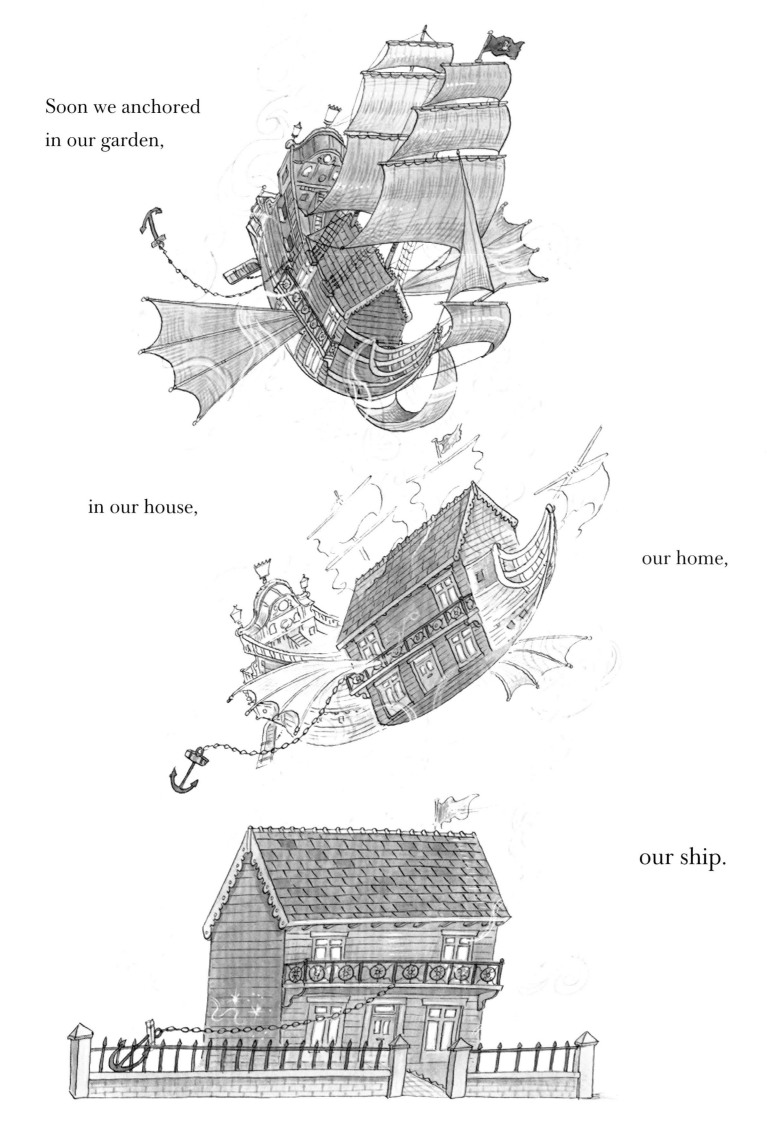

Parents tiptoed in and found us
sitting on the kitchen tiles.
We were terrified they'd ground us.
Not this time. They were all smiles.

"Long John told us that, as kids go,
you're the cream of any crop!"
Then they spied two dinner bowls
untouched upon the countertop.

My mum said, "Gosh. That smells like stew
and we are both still peckish here."
We told them, "No, they aren't for you.
They're more or less a souvenir."

"What luck!" cried Mum. "Oh good!" said Dad.
"A late-night snack is what we need!"
"Our meal tonight was very bad."
"Let's snack," said Dad. Said Mum, "Let's feed."

We yelled, "That's what you must **not** do!"

Too late! As one they spooned and scoffed.

"Yum, yum," they said. "It's scrumptious stew . . ."

"Now, hoist the **pirate** flag aloft!"

And that is why, since then, we've had
a Pirate Mum and Pirate Dad.

Pirate Stew! Pirate Stew!
Pirate Stew for me and you!

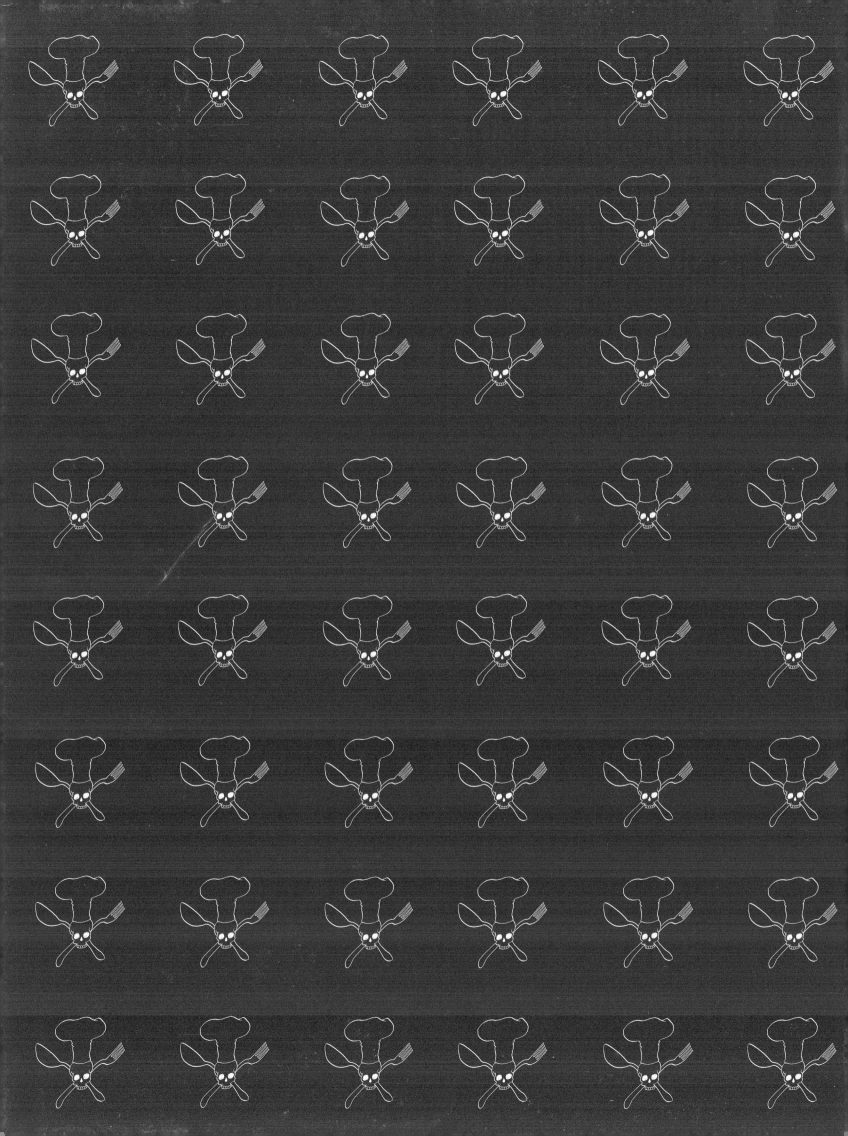